INSPIRING STORIES

For Brave Girls

THIS B♡♡K
BEL♡NGS TO:

_____

_____

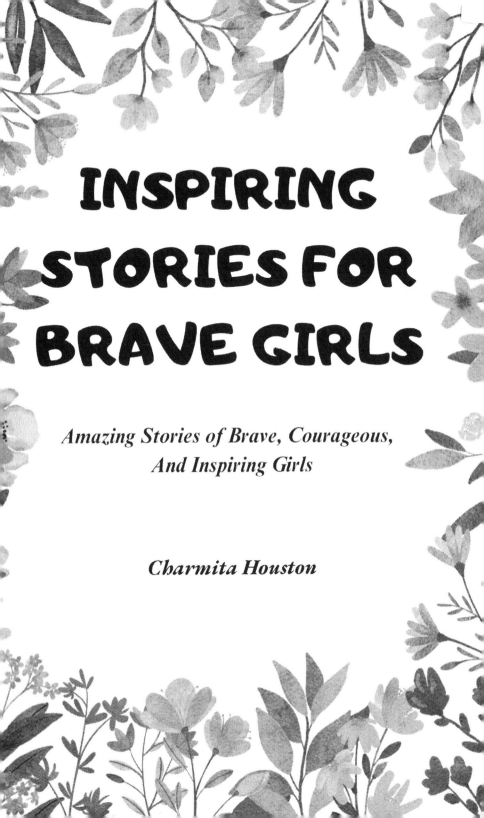

INSPIRING STORIES FOR BRAVE GIRLS

Amazing Stories of Brave, Courageous, And Inspiring Girls

Charmita Houston

CONTENT

INTRODUCTION

Welcome to "Inspiring Stories For Brave Girls," a collection of amazing stories of bravery, courage, determination, and inspiring girls. This book is dedicated to all the brave girls out there who are determined to break barriers and pursue their dreams.

Each chapter in this book focuses on different themes such as defying gender norms, standing up to bullies and empowering others. In addition, it features stories of girls who overcame adversity, fought for justice, and blazed trails in STEM fields. These stories will inspire young girls to pursue their passions, navigate their cultural identities, and heal from trauma.

In "Overcoming Fear," you will read about girls who faced their fears and pushed past their limitations. "Pursuing Passion" showcases stories of girls who pursued their dreams against all odds, while "Forgiveness and Reconciliation" feature stories of girls who forgave and reconciled with those who wronged them.

The stories in this book highlight the courage and resilience of girls who overcame illness, disability, and cultural barriers. In "Healing From Trauma," you will read about girls who overcame the darkest moments of their lives and found hope and strength.

This book is a celebration of the power of girls and their determination to make a difference in the world. It is a testament to the fact that girls can be anything they want to be, and nothing can stop them from achieving their dreams. So, get ready to be inspired, empowered, and motivated by the stories of these brave girls.

OVERCOMING ADVERSITY

OVERCOMING ADVERSITY

In the small village of Kibera, the sound of children laughing and playing echoed through the dirt paths that led to their homes. But not everyone in the village had reason to smile. Among them was a young girl named Aisha. She had faced incredible challenges and obstacles in her life, but despite all odds, she had persevered and succeeded.

Aisha's story began when she was just five years old. Her parents, who were struggling to make ends meet, could no longer afford to keep her in school. Aisha, who loved learning, was devastated. But she refused to let this setback keep her down.

Instead, Aisha started spending her days at the library, devouring book after book. She read about history, science, and mathematics and practiced her writing and arithmetic in the margins of her notebooks. She even taught herself to speak English, a language that was not spoken in her village.

But Aisha's challenges were far from over. One day, when she was walking home from the library, she was attacked by a group of bullies. They laughed at her for her love of learning and for her dream of becoming a doctor. They taunted her, telling her that girls like her had no place in the world of medicine.

Aisha was heartbroken. She had never felt so alone and defeated. But she refused to give up.

She knew that she had a calling and a purpose, and she was determined to achieve it.

So Aisha worked harder than ever before. She studied for hours each day, even after the sun went down and her village was plunged into darkness. She practiced her English with anyone who would listen and even started teaching the younger children in her village.

And slowly but surely, Aisha's hard work paid off. She was accepted into a prestigious school for girls, where she continued to excel academically. She volunteered at a local clinic, where she gained invaluable medical knowledge and experience. And eventually, she was accepted into medical school.

It wasn't easy, but Aisha never lost faith in herself.

She knew she had the power to overcome any obstacle and was willing to do whatever it took to achieve her dreams.

Now, as a successful doctor, Aisha gives back to her community in countless ways. She mentors young girls who, like her, dream of pursuing careers in medicine. She volunteers at the local clinic, providing medical care to those who cannot afford it. And she speaks out against bullying, hoping to inspire others to believe in themselves and pursue their passions.

WHAT DID I LEARN?

THOUGHTS I DON'T WANT TO FORGET:

DEFYING GENDER NORMS

DEFYING GENDER NORMS

The sky was ablaze with colors as the sun began to set over the bustling city. Amid the hustle and bustle was a young girl named Maya. From a young age, Maya had always felt a burning desire to challenge traditional gender roles and societal expectations, breaking down barriers and paving the way for others.

Maya's journey began when she was just a child. Her parents had always encouraged her to play with dolls and wear pretty dresses, but Maya had other ideas. She wanted to play soccer and climb trees, and she didn't care what anyone else thought.

At school, Maya faced ridicule and discrimination from her classmates. They told her that girls couldn't play sports or climb trees and that they were supposed to be pretty and delicate. But Maya refused to listen. Instead, she practiced her soccer skills every day, determined to prove them wrong.

And slowly but surely, Maya began to make progress. She joined a local soccer team and quickly became the star player. Her skills were unmatched, and her passion for the game was contagious. Soon, other girls began to follow in her footsteps, challenging gender norms and breaking down barriers.

But Maya's journey was far from over. As she grew older, she realized that there were even more obstacles to overcome. Maya faced discrimination and unequal pay in the workplace simply because of her gender.

But she refused to back down. Instead, she worked hard and earned a degree in engineering, breaking down yet another barrier and paving the way for other girls in the field.

Now, as a successful engineer and soccer coach, Maya continues to inspire young girls to challenge gender norms and pursue their passions. She speaks out against discrimination and inequality, and she works to create a world where everyone has the chance to thrive, regardless of their gender.

WHAT DID I LEARN?

THOUGHTS I DON'T WANT TO FORGET:

STANDING UP TO BULLIES

STANDING UP TO BULLIES

As the school bell rang, Maria felt her stomach tighten with dread. She knew what was coming: the daily torment from the bullies in her class. They called her names, made fun of her clothes, and even pushed her around on the playground. Maria tried to ignore them and focus on her studies, but it was becoming harder and harder to keep up her façade of strength.

One day, as Maria was walking home from school, she heard a commotion in the park. As she approached, she saw a group of younger kids being bullied by a group of older boys.

Maria felt a pang of empathy for the younger children and knew she had to do something.

With all the courage she could muster, Maria stepped forward and confronted the bullies. At first, they laughed and taunted her, but Maria stood her ground. She told them that what they were doing was wrong and hurtful and that they needed to stop.

To Maria's surprise, the bullies backed down and left the park. The younger children thanked her and went home, feeling safer and more protected. Maria walked home feeling empowered and proud of herself for standing up to the bullies.

The next day at school, the bullies tried to taunt Maria as usual, but she stood up to them and told them that their behavior was unacceptable. To her surprise, some of her classmates who had been watching the situation play out spoke up and defended Maria. They too had been bullied by the same group and were inspired by Maria's bravery to speak up and stand up for what was right.

Maria became a leader in her class, organizing anti-bullying campaigns and encouraging others to speak out against bullying. She knew that it was important to create a safe and supportive community where everyone felt valued and respected.

Over time, the school became a much better place to be, with less bullying and more positivity.

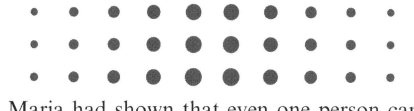

Maria had shown that even one person can make a difference and that standing up for what is right is always worth it.

WHAT DID I LEARN?

THOUGHTS I DON'T WANT TO FORGET:

EMPOWERING
OTHERS

EMPOWERING OTHERS

It was a sunny day, and birds sang in the trees. Amid this idyllic scene was a young girl named Lily. Lily was not your average girl; she had a heart of gold and a burning desire to impact the world positively.

From a young age, Lily had always been passionate about helping others. She would spend her free time volunteering at the local soup kitchen and collecting donations for the less fortunate. Her parents were proud of her and encouraged her to pursue her dreams of positively impacting the world.

As she grew older, Lily began to develop her talents and resources.

She learned to bake and started selling her delicious treats to raise money for charity. She also started a small enterprise selling handmade crafts to raise money for various causes. Her dedication and hard work paid off, and she soon raised thousands of dollars for organizations that helped people in need.

But Lily's journey was not without challenges. She faced criticism from people who didn't understand her passion for helping others. They told her that she should focus on her own life and leave the problems of the world to someone else. But Lily refused to listen. She knew that she had a responsibility to use her talents and resources to make a positive impact in the world.

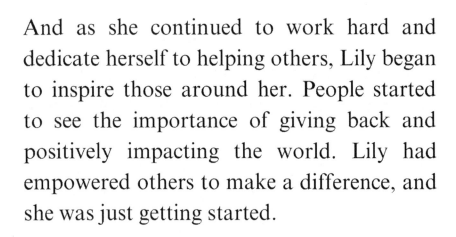

And as she continued to work hard and dedicate herself to helping others, Lily began to inspire those around her. People started to see the importance of giving back and positively impacting the world. Lily had empowered others to make a difference, and she was just getting started.

Today, Lily continues to inspire people around the world with her dedication and passion for making a positive impact in the world. She has traveled to different countries to help people in need, and she has started her own non-profit organization to help those who are less fortunate. Her legacy will live on, inspiring generations to come to use their talents and resources to make a difference in the world.

WHAT DID I LEARN?

THOUGHTS I DON'T WANT TO FORGET:

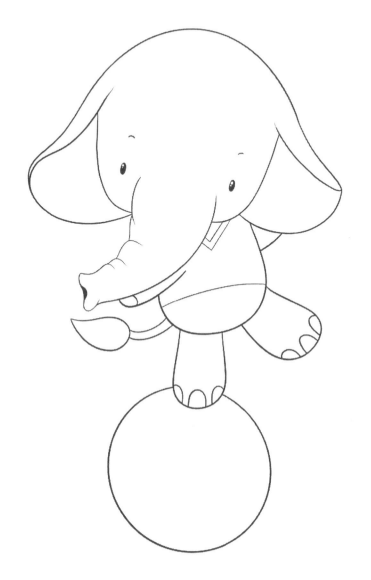

TRAILBLAZING IN STEM

TRAILBLAZING IN STEM

Deep in the heart of the city, a young girl named Maya sat hunched over her desk, furiously scribbling away in her notebook. Her eyes were fixed on the screen of her computer as she typed away, her fingers dancing across the keyboard with lightning-fast speed.

Maya had always been fascinated by the world of science, technology, engineering, and mathematics, or STEM for short. She loved exploring the mysteries of the universe and uncovering the natural world's secrets. And as she grew older, she realized that she had a special talent for understanding the complex systems and processes that underpinned our world.

But Maya's journey was a challenging one. She faced obstacles at every turn, from people who didn't believe in her abilities to a lack of resources and support. But Maya refused to give up. She knew that she had a passion for STEM that could change the world, and she was determined to see it through.

Through hard work, dedication, and sheer force of will, Maya excelled in STEM. She won countless awards and accolades, and her groundbreaking research made headlines around the world. Maya had become a trailblazer in STEM, paving the way for future generations of young girls to follow in her footsteps.

But Maya's greatest achievement was not in her research or her accolades.

It was in the way that she inspired and empowered others. She mentored young girls who were starting out in STEM, sharing her knowledge and expertise with them and encouraging them to pursue their dreams. And she used her platform to speak out about the importance of inclusivity and diversity in STEM, advocating for a world where everyone had the opportunity to pursue their passions and positively impact the world.

Maya's legacy lives on today, inspiring young girls around the globe to pursue their passions and make a difference in STEM. Her tale is a testament to the power of perseverance, dedication, and unwavering belief in oneself.

WHAT DID I LEARN?

THOUGHTS I DON'T WANT TO FORGET:

FIGHTING FOR
JUSTICE

FIGHTING FOR JUSTICE

The sun was setting over the city as a young girl named Aisha sat huddled on her porch, lost in thought. She had just returned from a protest march, where she and hundreds of others had taken to the streets to demand justice for marginalized and oppressed communities.

Aisha had always been passionate about fighting for what was right. She had seen firsthand the injustices and inequalities that existed in the world, and she knew that she had a duty to stand up and speak out against them.

And so, she began to dedicate her life to fighting for justice.

She attended protests and rallies, wrote letters to politicians and policymakers, and spoke out on social media and in public forums. She became a tireless advocate for the rights of marginalized and oppressed communities, working tirelessly to create a fair and just world for all.

But Aisha's journey was not without its challenges. She faced opposition from those who disagreed with her views, and she sometimes felt discouraged by the slow pace of progress. But she refused to give up. She knew that the fight for justice was long and difficult, but she also knew it was a fight worth fighting.

Over time, Aisha's advocacy began to pay off.

She saw changes happening, albeit slowly, and she felt a sense of fulfillment and accomplishment in knowing that she had played a role in making the world a better place.

Today, Aisha continues to fight for justice, using her platform to raise awareness about the issues that matter most to her. Her tale is a testament to the power of speaking out and standing up for what is right, even in the face of opposition and adversity.

WHAT DID I LEARN?

THOUGHTS I DON'T WANT TO FORGET:

OVERCOMING FEAR

OVERCOMING FEAR

There was once a young girl named Ava who was terrified of heights. She would never go on roller coasters or even climb a ladder to reach high shelves. But Ava's fear of heights did not stop her from dreaming of becoming a pilot.

One day, Ava's school announced a competition where the winner would get to take a ride in a hot air balloon. Ava's friends encouraged her to participate, but she was hesitant. Eventually, Ava gathered the courage to sign up for the competition, hoping it would help her overcome her fear of heights.

The day of the competition arrived, and Ava was shaking with nerves as she watched the hot air balloon rise up into the sky. But as she looked up, Ava realized something - the view from above was breathtaking. She could see the world from a whole new perspective.

Ava ended up winning the competition and got to take a ride in the hot air balloon. From that day on, she became determined to face her fear of heights and pursue her dream of becoming a pilot. She started by taking small steps, like climbing a ladder to reach high shelves or going on a Ferris wheel. Slowly but surely, Ava's fear began to diminish, and she gained more confidence in herself.

Eventually, Ava enrolled in a flight school and worked hard to earn her pilot's license. She faced many challenges along the way, but her determination and courage helped her push through. Today, Ava is a successful pilot, flying planes and traveling the world.

WHAT DID I LEARN?

THOUGHTS I DON'T WANT TO FORGET:

PURSUING PASSION

PURSUING PASSION

Once there was a girl named Maya who had a deep passion for music. From a young age, Maya was drawn to different instruments and would spend hours practicing and experimenting with different sounds. Her parents, however, were skeptical of her passion and encouraged her to focus on more practical pursuits.

Despite this, Maya refused to give up on her dreams. She saved up money from odd jobs to buy her own guitar and started performing at local coffee shops and open mic nights. Maya's talent was quickly recognized, and she was invited to perform at larger venues and festivals.

However, as Maya's career began to take off, she faced criticism and sexism from industry professionals who believed that women couldn't succeed in the music industry. Maya refused to let this discourage her and continued to work hard, constantly improving her skills and collaborating with other musicians.

Eventually, Maya's dedication paid off, and she was offered a recording contract with a major label. Her music spoke to people around the world, and she became a role model for young girls who dreamed of pursuing their passions.

WHAT DID I LEARN?

THOUGHTS I DON'T WANT TO FORGET:

NAVIGATING CULTURAL IDENTITY

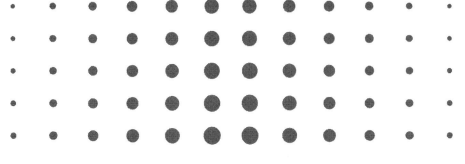

NAVIGATING CULTURAL IDENTITY

Once upon a time, in a small town, there was a young girl named Aisha. Aisha was a first-generation immigrant from a South Asian country, and she often struggled to navigate her cultural identity in her new home. She was torn between her family's traditions and the modern Western lifestyle that surrounded her.

Aisha felt like she was constantly walking on a tightrope, trying to balance both worlds. She was teased at school for the food she brought for lunch and the way she dressed, and she felt like she didn't fit in anywhere.

Aisha wanted to find a way to embrace her cultural identity without feeling like an outsider in her own community.

One day, Aisha's grandmother came to visit from her home country. She shared stories with Aisha about their family's history, their traditions, and the struggles they had faced in their journey to the United States. Aisha was fascinated and felt a newfound sense of pride in her roots.

With her grandmother's guidance, Aisha began to explore her cultural identity in more depth. She learned to cook traditional dishes, practiced her family's religious customs, and even started to wear clothing that reflected her heritage.

Aisha found that the more she embraced her culture, the more confident she felt in her own skin.

But Aisha's journey was not without its challenges. She faced backlash from some of her peers and even some members of her own family who didn't understand why she was making these changes. However, Aisha knew that this was the right path for her and that it was important for her to stay true to herself.

As Aisha grew older, she became an advocate for cultural understanding and diversity. She started a club at her school to celebrate and educate others about different cultures and traditions.

She also worked with her family to create a nonprofit organization that supported immigrant families in their community.

Through her journey, Aisha learned that embracing her cultural identity was not about choosing one world over the other but about finding a way to bring the two together. She realized that her unique perspective was a strength and that she could use it to make a positive impact in the world.

WHAT DID I LEARN?

THOUGHTS I DON'T WANT TO FORGET:

HEALING FROM
TRAUMA

HEALING FROM TRAUMA

Once upon a time, there was a girl named Maya. She was just like any other girl her age, with a contagious smile and a love for adventure. But Maya had experienced something that no child should ever have to endure - she had been through a traumatic experience that left her feeling scared, alone, and confused.

Maya's journey to healing was not an easy one. She struggled to make sense of what had happened to her and to find a way to move forward. But through her own strength and the support of loved ones, Maya slowly began to heal.

One of the things that helped Maya the most was finding ways to express herself. She loved to draw, and she found that when she put pen to paper, she was able to let out some of the emotions that had been bottled up inside. Maya also started writing in a journal, and through this practice, she was able to reflect on her experiences and gain a deeper understanding of her own feelings.

As Maya continued on her healing journey, she realized that she wanted to help others who had been through similar experiences. She began volunteering at a local organization that provided support for survivors of trauma, and she found that by listening to other's stories and sharing her own, she was able to make a real difference in their lives.

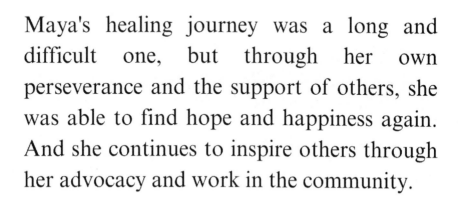

Maya's healing journey was a long and difficult one, but through her own perseverance and the support of others, she was able to find hope and happiness again. And she continues to inspire others through her advocacy and work in the community.

WHAT DID I LEARN?

THOUGHTS I DON'T WANT TO FORGET:

OVERCOMING ILLNESS OR DISABILITY

OVERCOMING ILLNESS OR DISABILITY

There was a girl named Asa who had a passion for dance. From a young age, she was always moving to the beat, twirling around the living room, and choreographing her own routines. However, at the age of six, Asa was diagnosed with juvenile arthritis, which caused her joints to swell and become painful, making it difficult for her to move and dance.

Asa was devastated. She felt like her dreams of becoming a professional dancer were shattered, and she didn't know how she could continue to pursue her passion while dealing with her condition.

Her parents encouraged her to see a specialist, who recommended physical therapy and medication to manage her symptoms.

Asa was determined not to let her illness stop her from dancing. She worked hard with her physical therapist to strengthen her muscles and improve her flexibility. She also started taking medication to manage her arthritis, which helped to reduce her pain.

Asa slowly began to regain her strength and flexibility, and she started to dance again. She had to modify some of her movements to accommodate her condition, but she never gave up on her passion. Asa's love for dance was so strong that she found ways to adapt to her illness and continued to pursue her dreams.

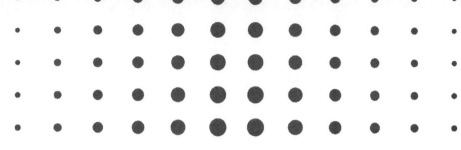

As she grew older, Asa became a role model for other girls with disabilities who also loved dance. She started a dance program for kids with physical disabilities and became an advocate for inclusive dance education. Asa showed that even with a disability, you can still achieve your dreams and make a difference in the world.

WHAT DID I LEARN?

THOUGHTS I DON'T WANT TO FORGET:

FORGIVENESS AND RECONCILIATION

FORGIVENESS AND RECONCILIATION

Mia had always been close to her best friend, Ava. They met in kindergarten and have been inseparable ever since. They did everything together: playing dress-up, baking cupcakes, and going on adventures. However, things started to change when they got older. In middle school, Ava joined a popular clique and began to distance herself from Mia. She stopped inviting her to parties and didn't have time for their usual hangouts.

Mia was hurt and confused, but she didn't understand what she had done wrong.

She tried to talk to Ava about it, but Ava would roll her eyes and say that Mia was too boring for her new friends. Mia felt like she had lost her best friend and didn't know what to do.

One day, Mia was walking home from school when she saw Ava crying on a bench. She approached her, hesitant at first, but Ava seemed to be genuinely upset. She had gotten into a fight with her new friends, and they had said some hurtful things to her. Mia sat down next to Ava, and they started talking.

At first, Ava was defensive and blamed everyone else for her problems.

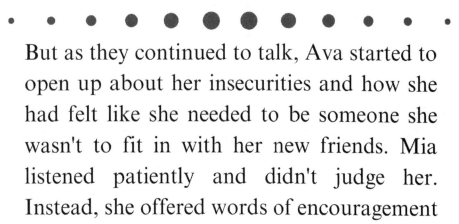

But as they continued to talk, Ava started to open up about her insecurities and how she had felt like she needed to be someone she wasn't to fit in with her new friends. Mia listened patiently and didn't judge her. Instead, she offered words of encouragement and support.

It wasn't easy, but Mia and Ava worked through their issues and were able to reconcile. They both had to learn to forgive each other and let go of past hurts. It was a journey that required patience, understanding, and empathy, but it was worth it.

Through their experience, Mia learned that forgiveness and reconciliation are powerful tools that can help heal relationships and mend broken bonds.

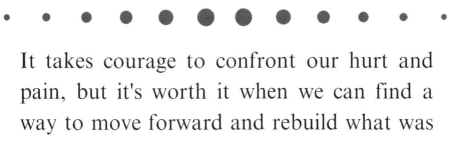

It takes courage to confront our hurt and pain, but it's worth it when we can find a way to move forward and rebuild what was lost.

WHAT DID I LEARN?

THOUGHTS I DON'T WANT TO FORGET:

Notes

Date: _____

_____
_____
_____
_____
_____
_____
_____
_____
_____
_____
_____
_____
_____
_____
_____
_____
_____
_____
_____
_____
_____
_____
_____
_____
_____
_____
_____
_____

Notes

Date : _____

_____
_____
_____
_____
_____
_____
_____
_____
_____
_____
_____
_____
_____
_____
_____
_____
_____
_____
_____
_____
_____
_____
_____
_____

Notes

Date :

Printed in Great Britain
by Amazon

33502464R00062